SATURDAY MORNING LASTS FOREVER

Elizabeth Bram

The Dial Press • New York

The Dial Press
One Dag Hammarskjold Plaza
New York, New York 10017

Typography by Atha Tehon

Library of Congress Cataloging in Publication Data
Bram, Elizabeth.
Saturday morning lasts forever.
Summary: While Susan's parents sleep late one Saturday
morning she finds various ways to occupy herself.
I. Title.
PZ7.B7357Sat   [E]   78-51318
ISBN 0-8037-7627-6
ISBN 0-8037-7628-4 lib. bdg.

For Connie

Susan woke up early on Saturday morning.

She tiptoed into her parents' room,

but they were sound asleep.

She went outside to talk to her dog.

The sun had been up
for hours and there was
a new bird in their yard.

She went for a walk

and picked flowers.

She lay in the grass
and watched the clouds
turn into faces.

She collected old bottle caps
and bits of colored paper,

and put them in an old cigar box
that smelled like her Uncle Jack.

When she got back,
her parents were still asleep.
They did not even hear the
bedroom door creak open and shut.

She went next door to watch
Mrs. Fox hang out the laundry.

"Are your mother and father
sleeping late this morning?"
Mrs. Fox asked. Susan nodded.

"You can come and have breakfast
with me if you like," she said.

So Susan had breakfast with Mrs. Fox.

Afterward she returned home.
But her parents were still asleep.

They did not hear her
thump in and out of their room.

So Susan drew pictures
with colored chalk

and watched some ants
crawling along the sidewalk.

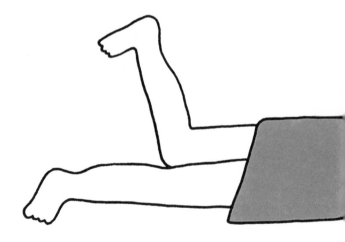

Then suddenly she heard
her dog barking.

She ran into the bedroom
and found her mother and father
finally waking up.

"Is it time for breakfast?"
asked her mother
as Susan jumped up on the bed.

"No," said Susan. "It's time for lunch.